A Unicorn Miracle The Story of Hanukkah

In the Holy Land
A long time ago
A lovely king
Sat on his throne

He was kind to the Jews
Let's say they're unicorns
And would let them pray
And blow their rams horns

But one day he died
Which was very sad
So his son became king
And he was really bad.

Antiochus was his name
He was an Assyrian Greek
He didn't like Unicorns
He thought they were weak.

So he gathered his troops
All of his fellow horses
And told them to unite
They were his armed forces.

"I want you to spy
and I want you to sneak
To watch those Unicorns"
are the words he did speak.

"Make sure the Unicorns
Don't learn from their Torah
or sing all their prayers
Or light the Menorah"

An announcement was sent
All over the town
About the Kings new rules
Which made the Unicorns frown.

One Unicorn - Mattathias
Let's just call him Matt
Stood up and shouted
"I'm not having that!"

"We have to stand up"
He said to his crew
"Do not be ashamed
of being a Jew!"

They formed their own army
The Maccabees they were called
All the Assyrian Horses
Were really appalled.

They learned in secret
And played with spin tops
To hide all their learning
From the King's cops.

Then Matt's son Judah
took charge of the group
assembled more Unicorns
To fight the King's troops.

The king, meanwhile
Sent his troops on a mission
To go into the temple
and ruin its condition.

They entered the Temple
relieved that they won
They searched for some oil
but it seemed there was none.

"We can't light it now!"
The Jews all cried
we need to look more
Search far and wide.

And after a while
in a mess on the floor
A small bottle was found
"But isn't there more?"

To make more oil
Will take eight days
Let's start with this
and everyone pray

The menorah stayed shining
Long after day one
No one expected it
To stay lit for so long.

The Menorah stayed burning
And on day eight
They now had new oil
And said "let's celebrate!"

The Jews danced and sang
There was joy in the air
"Ness Gadol Haya Sham"
A Great Miracle Happened There.

Enjoyed this book?
Please consider leaving a review

Would you like to receive free Judaism Activity and coloring pages? Scan the QR code below!

www.yellowsunpublishing.com